This book belongs to

Samantha

Reading together

This book is designed to be fun for children who are just starting to read on their own. They will enjoy and benefit from some time discussing the stories with an adult. Encourage them to pause and talk about what is happening in the pictures. Help them to spot familiar words and sound out the letters in harder words. Look at the following ways you can help your child take those first steps in reading:

Explore the stories

Make the most of each page by talking about the pictures and spotting key words. Encourage your child to sound out the letters in any words he or she does not know. Look at the common "key" words listed at the end of the story and see which of them your child can find on each page.

Test understanding

It is one thing to understand one word at a time, but it is important to make sure your child can understand the stories as a whole!

Ask your child questions as you read each story, for example:

- Who is Jaffa?
- What do the aliens give to Lola?
- Do you like Lola's shop?
- What is wrong with Lola's big top?

Play "find the obvious mistake." Read the text as your child looks at the words with you, but make an obvious mistake to see if he or she catches it. Ask your child to correct you and provide the right word.

Activity sections

A "Ready to Tell" section at the end of each story encourages children to remember what happened and retell the story. The picture dictionary pages help children to increase their vocabulary, and the useful word pages reinforce their knowledge of the most common words. There is also a "Lola and her friends" section where children can learn about all of Lola the Lollipop Fairy's friends!

Lola the
Lollipop Fairy

Lola's Lollipopper Showstopper and other stories

Lola the
Lollipop Fairy

Lola's Lollipop Shop

Lola has a new lollipop shop.

Lollipop
Shop

This way
→

"My lollipop shop is by the big top," says Lola.

Lola's
Lollipop Shop

Lola sells lollipops
in every color.

The lollipops are different
sizes, but they are all yummy!

At nine o'clock,
Lola opens her shop.
All the fairies come to
buy her lovely lollipops.

Lovely
Lollipops

Linda buys a blue one.
Lulu buys a red one.

"May I please have three lollipops?" says Lisa.

At five o'clock, Lola
runs out of lollipops!

Lovely
Lollipops

After tea, Lola makes more lollipops to sell in her shop tomorrow.

In the evening, Lola, Linda, and Lulu perform their circus show!

Ready to tell

Can you remember what happened in the story? Look at each picture and try retelling the story.

4

5

6

7

23

Lola's fairy dictionary

shop

red

circus show

clock

blue

three

Lola's useful words

Here are some key words used in context. Make simple sentences for the other words in the border.

This is Lola. **She** has a lollipop shop.

The fairies **come** to the shop.

Lisa buys lots **of** lollipops.

Lola closes **her** shop at five o'clock.

Lola makes **many** lollipops to sell.

Lola's Big Top Bother

Lola, Linda, and Lulu
are excited about the
circus show tonight!

The fairies are practicing
in the big top. The big top
is old and full of holes.

Linda lifts her weights.
It starts to rain. Linda
gets wet!

Lulu spins her plates.
The wind blows
through the roof.

The wind blows the plates
off the poles!

Lola juggles lollipops, but they fly through the roof!

The fairies need
a new big top.

Lola has a great idea.
Lola, Linda, and Lulu
get ready for a very
special show.

The special show is very
exciting. Lola flies to
the moon!

Lots of fairies come to see the new show. Now the fairies can buy a beautiful, new big top!

Ready to tell

Can you remember what happened
in the story? Look at each picture
and try retelling the story.

1

2

3

4

5

6

7

8

45

Lola's fairy dictionary

big top

wind

rain

weights

plate

juggle

Lola's useful words

Here are some key words used in context. Make simple sentences for the other words in the border.

The big top **is** old.

The fairies practice **for** their show.

The wind blows the plates **away**.

Lola has **an** idea.

The fairies get a new **big** top.

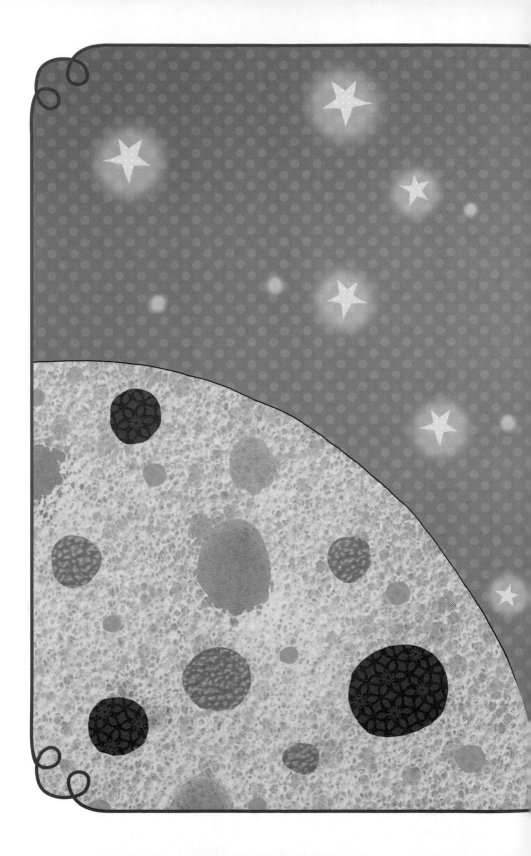

Lola is ready to fly to
the moon. She puts on
her glasses and circus hat.

Lola waves good-bye
to her pet cat, Jaffa.

She zooms up
into the sky.

53

"The moon looks like a big lollipop!" says Lola.

55

There are aliens on the moon.
They are small and green.

57

Lola plays and dances
with the aliens all day.
"I wish I could stay,"
says Lola.

It is nearly six o'clock!
Lola has to get home for
her special circus show.

62

"Please take this special
lollipop as a gift from us,"
say the aliens.
"Thank you," says Lola.

Lola flies back home.
"Good-bye, Moon,"
says Lola. "See you soon!"

Ready to tell

Can you remember what happened in the story? Look at each picture and try retelling the story.

1

2

3

4

5

6

7

Lola's fairy dictionary

alien

cat

dance

moon

fly

lollipop

Lola's useful words

Here are some key words used in context. Make simple sentences for the other words in the border.

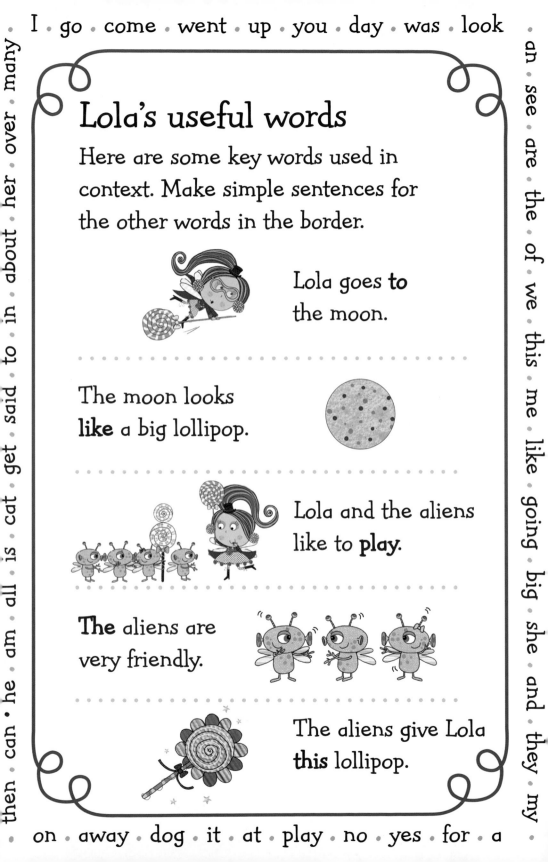

Lola goes **to** the moon.

The moon looks **like** a big lollipop.

Lola and the aliens like to **play**.

The aliens are very friendly.

The aliens give Lola **this** lollipop.

Lola wakes up. She is excited about the circus show tonight!

Linda and Lulu are hard
at work. They are getting
ready for the circus show.

Before the show, the fairies
go to the busy fairy salon.

Linda and Lulu put on
their circus dresses.

Lola and her pet cat,
Jaffa, put on their
special circus hats.

Lots of fairies are waiting
outside. They are excited
to see the circus show!

The cannon is ready.
The lights glow!
The circus show
is about to start.

Lola says, "Hello and welcome, everyone!" Lola, Linda, and Lulu perform their circus tricks.

At the end of the show, Lola flies high in the sky. She waves to the crowd and shouts, "Good-bye!"

Ready to tell

Can you remember what happened in the story? Look at each picture and try retelling the story.

1

2

3

4

5

6

7

89

Lola's fairy dictionary

hat

dress

lights

salon

cannon

crowd

Lola's useful words

Here are some key words used in context. Make simple sentences for the other words in the border.

Lola loves her **cat.**

The fairies **go** to the salon.

Jaffa puts **on** his circus hat.

The fairies **are** excited.

Lola flies **up** into the sky.

Lola and her friends

Lola is in charge
of the circus show.
Lola likes to think
of new ideas, such
as her lollipop shop!
Linda and Lulu are
her sisters.

Linda performs
in the circus show
with Lulu and Lola.
Linda is a weight lifter.
She also likes to sing
and dance!

Lulu spins plates
in the circus show.
Sometimes she
juggles lollipops too!

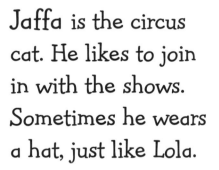

Jaffa is the circus
cat. He likes to join
in with the shows.
Sometimes he wears
a hat, just like Lola.

Morris the mouse is
Jaffa's best friend. He is
very nosy! Morris likes
to know what is going
on at all times.

Lisa is Lola's friend and she loves lollipops! Sometimes she performs exciting tricks in Lola's circus show.

Lara is Linda's friend. She performs on the flying trapeze at Lola's circus. She is very good at it!

Lily is Lisa's sister. She loves lollipops too! Lily's favorite lollipop flavor is lemon.

Lexi, Lulu's friend, loves the circus show. She likes Lola's cannon ride the best, and would really like to have a turn!